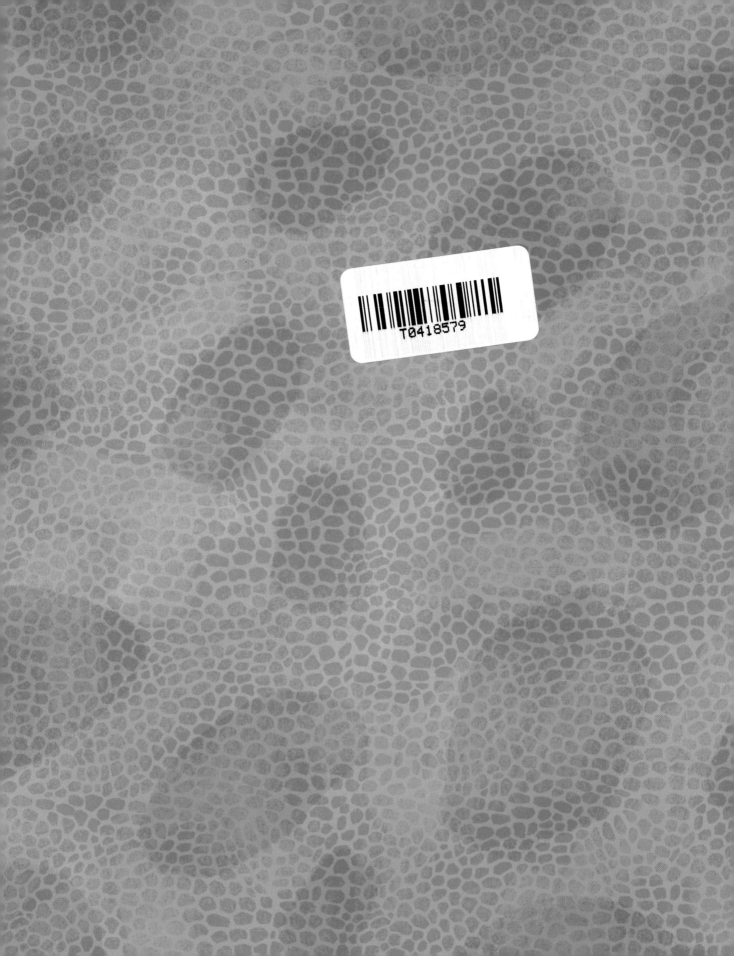

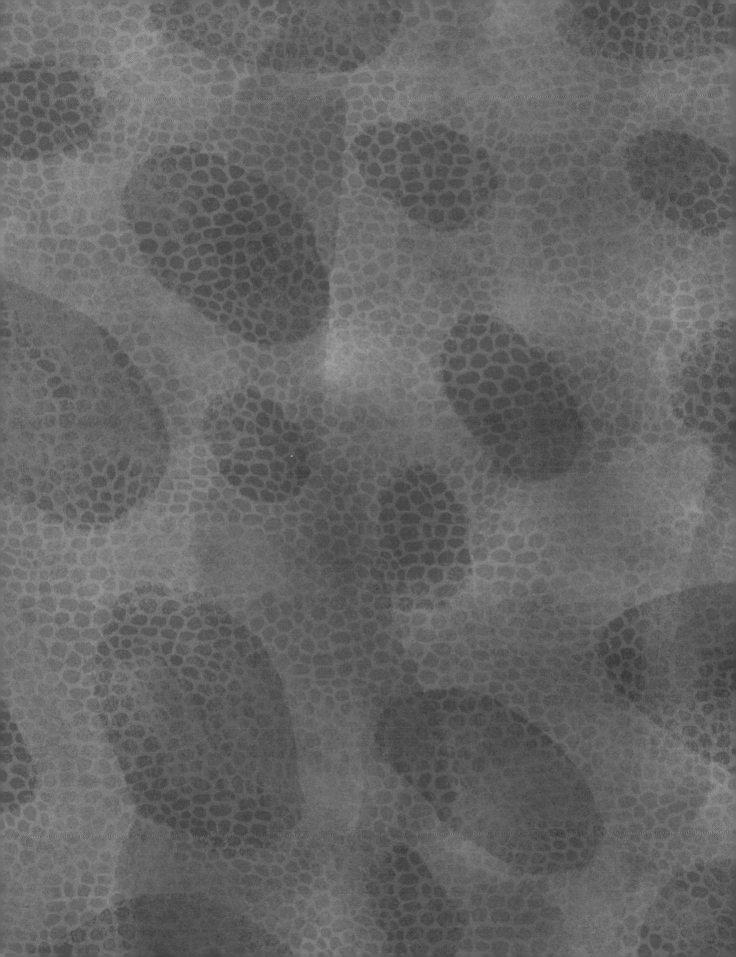

Calm Your ROAR Like a Dinosaur

For our dads—CAP & BSM

For Jack and Miles, my little dinosaurs—JJ

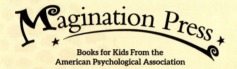

Text copyright ©2025 by Colleen A. Patterson and Brenda S. Miles. Illustrations copyright ©2025 by John Joseph. All rights reserved. Except as permitted under the United States Copyright Act of 1976, no part of this publication may be reproduced or distributed in any form or by any means, or stored in a database or retrieval system, without the prior written permission of the publisher.

Magination Press, Books for Kids From the American Psychological Association
maginationpress.org

Distributed by Lerner Publisher Services
lernerbooks.com

Book design by Christina Gaugler
Printed by Corporate Graphics, North Mankato, MN

Library of Congress Cataloging-in-Publication Data

Names: Patterson, Colleen A., author. | Miles, Brenda, author. | Joseph, John, 1985- illustrator.

Title: Calm your roar like a dinosaur / Colleen A. Patterson and Brenda S. Miles; illustrated by John Joseph.

Description: Washington: Magination Press, 2025. | American Psychological Association. | Summary: Dinosaurs calm their roar with Progressive Muscle Relaxation.—Provided by publisher.

Identifiers: LCCN 2024024865 (print) | LCCN 2024024866 (ebook) | ISBN 9781433844652 (hardcover) | ISBN 9781433844669 (ebook)

Subjects: CYAC: Dinosaurs—Fiction. | Muscles—Fiction. | Relaxation—Fiction. | Stretching exercises—Fiction. | LCGFT: Picture books.

Classification: LCC PZ7.1.P38 Cal 2025 (print) | LCC PZ7.1.P38 (ebook) | DDC [E]—dc23

LC record available at https://lccn.loc.gov/2024024865
LC ebook record available at https://lccn.loc.gov/2024024866

Manufactured in the United States of America

10 9 8 7 6 5 4 3 2 1

Calm Your ROAR Like a Dinosaur

How to Relax Muscle by Muscle

by Colleen A. Patterson and Brenda S. Miles

Illustrated by John Joseph

Magination Press • Washington, DC • American Psychological Association

Breathe in, breathe out, quiet and slow.

With gentle breaths,
 you're ready to go.

Now relax your neck to **calm the roar.**

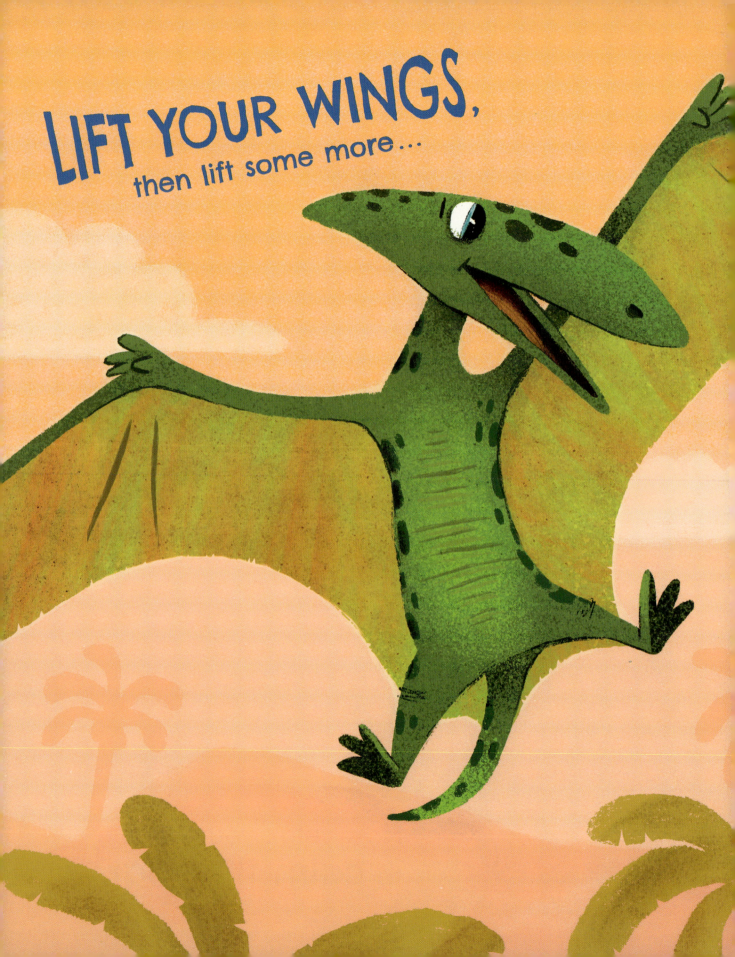

Now relax your wings to **calm the roar.**

Now relax your claws to **calm the roar.**

Now relax your belly to **calm the roar.**

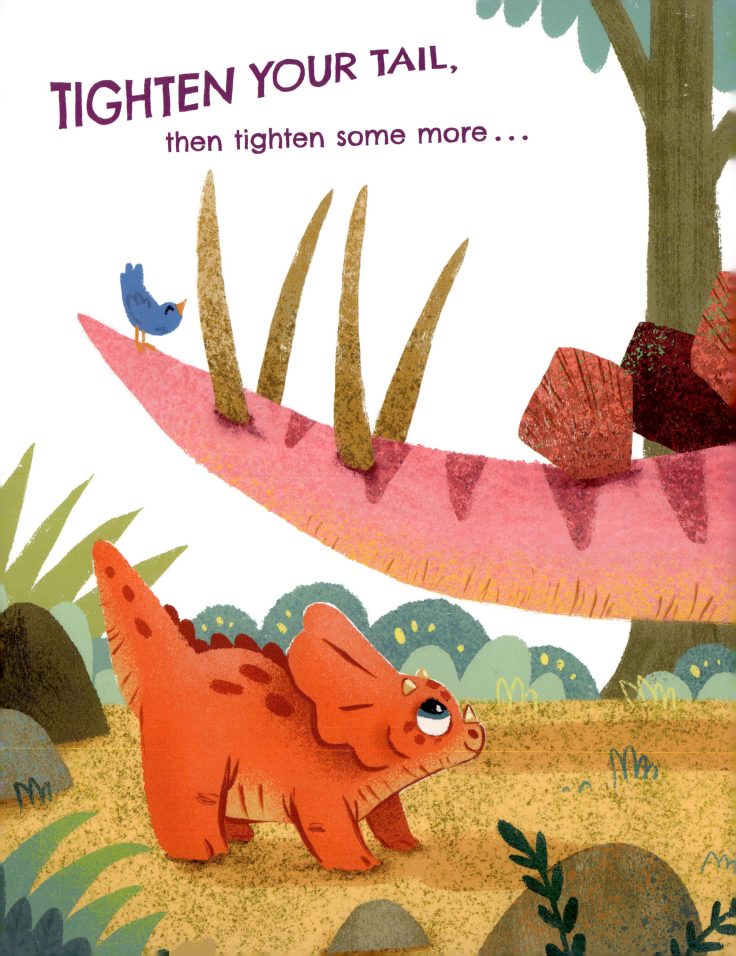

Now relax your tail to **calm the roar.**

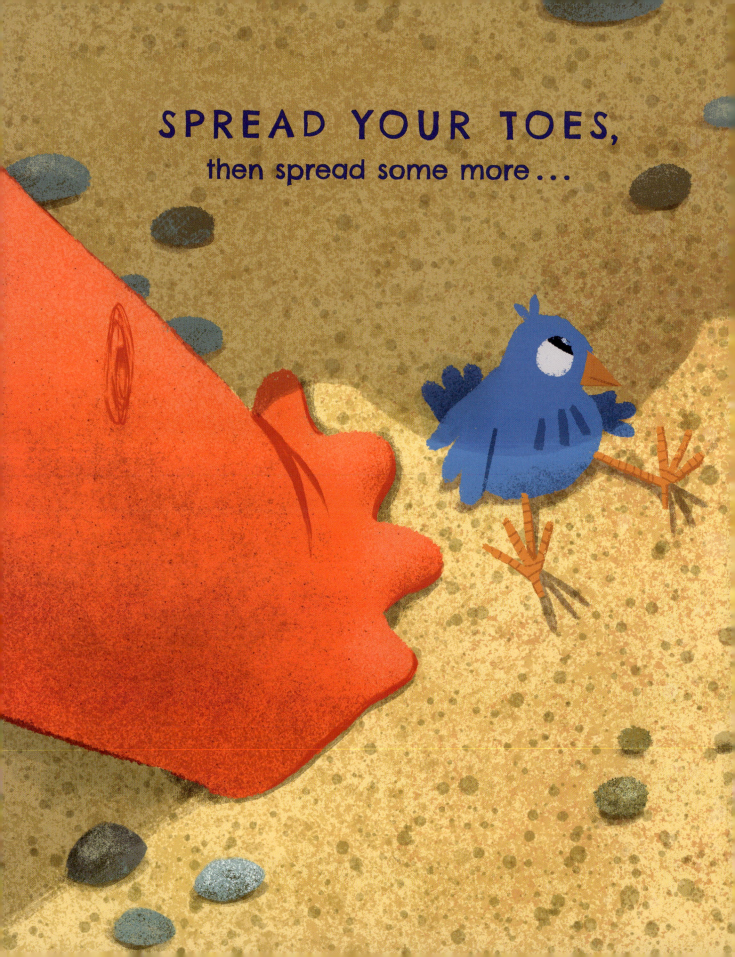

Now relax your toes to **calm the roar.**

Breathe in, breathe out,
you calmed your roar.

Reader's Note

At any age, humans experience stressful moments or events that have physical effects on the body. Psychologists talk about two kinds of stress: positive stress and negative stress. Positive stress can energize us, making us feel very excited. On the flip side, negative stress can drain us, making us feel very worried. Knowing what our body and mind need to reset, so we can feel more balanced or calm, is a skill called self-regulation. Progressive Muscle Relaxation (PMR) is a technique that can help individuals of all ages become aware of tension the body carries, and what it feels like to release that tension, so we can relax, reset, and find the balance we need.

Self-Regulation Develops Over Time

Humans learn to recognize and reduce tension they are experiencing as they mature. What do you do to help your child reset? Maybe you model gentle breathing or offer a tight hug until you feel your child's body relax. When you offer these techniques, you're helping to reset your child's physiological reaction. A body reset can help quiet the mind, too, bringing it back onboard for some supportive self-talk or effective problem solving. Progressive Muscle Relaxation (PMR) gives you a new technique to help calm your child while teaching another way to self-regulate.

Progressive Muscle Relaxation is a Body Scan With a Twist

If you practice mindful meditation, you're probably familiar with a body scan. As you sit or lie quietly, you scan your body mentally and slowly, noticing all the sensations you feel from head to toe. Progressive Muscle Relaxation also encourages a focus on parts of the body in a systematic order while taking note of physical sensations. But there's a big difference between a mindful body scan and Progressive Muscle Relaxation. In PMR, when your mind focuses on a body part, that's your cue to activate and tense specific muscles. Taking note of the feeling helps you recognize what tension feels like in different parts of the body. Then, after a few seconds, you release the tension and let the muscle group relax.

It's Okay to Add Your Own Twists

Progressive Muscle Relaxation scripts can vary. We've reduced the number of body parts in our story to simplify the script for young children. Feel free to add parts like eyebrows and shoulders for extra fun. Encourage variation in flexing, too. Some children may open their jaws wide, while others may stretch their mouth to show their teeth. Read the words in the story slowly so children have time to experience the tension in their bodies and the relaxation that comes from releasing that tension. In conversations about the book, discuss what tension feels like in different body parts. Does it feel tingly or heavy? Talk about what relaxation feels like, too. Does it feel squishy or floppy? Teaching moments with collaborative discussion are best done in times of calm, rather than in moments of high excitement or frustration.

Encourage Gentle Breathing

Add gentle breathing to support your child's muscle relaxation routine. Clinicians often discuss belly, or diaphragmatic, breathing: breathing in through the nose, which moves the stomach out, and out through the mouth, which moves the stomach in. At first, regulated breathing can be hard for children. Some get confused trying to coordinate the nose inhales with the mouth exhales. Add controlled breathing to PMR and children might find the coordination even harder, trying to synchronize their breathing with flexing and relaxing. Here's our advice from years of clinical practice with young children; don't overthink it. The goal is gentle, relaxed breathing. Maybe that means breathing only through the nose or only through the mouth to make coordination easier. Some children have chronically stuffy noses, making mouth breathing the only option. Go with what feels comfortable for your child. Encourage your child to breathe in a gentle rhythm without breaking the pattern: in and out, in and out. "Try your best not to break the pattern" has been a helpful instruction we use in our clinical work. If your child needs visual support to practice relaxed breathing, draw a rippling ocean wave or the head of a Triceratops with its wavy, bony frill. Encourage your child to breathe in while tracing up a wave with one finger and then to exhale while tracing down the wave. Don't make the waves too big. The goal is gentle in-and-out breathing over a stretch of small waves.

Get Creative Anytime, Anywhere

Progressive Muscle Relaxation can be done anytime, anywhere. It can be done standing, sitting, or lying down. Think of moments when you could read this book and perform the actions with your child. After school or during your child's bedtime routine might be good options. If you go through all the muscle groups covered here, you'll need some time to move through the story slowly. If time is limited, some on-the-spot support could be helpful. Encourage your child to focus on a few muscle groups—but not all—that can be flexed and relaxed quickly. Gentle breathing paired with some hand and leg flexions might be relaxing before stressful situations. The words, "calm your roar," could cue your child to begin some muscle flexing or relaxing. In classrooms, teachers may find it helpful to read the entire book at the start of the day or before transition times. As the day progresses, a teacher might announce, "Calm your roar," or "Relaxosaur!" to encourage students to tense one or two muscle groups on the spot and then release that tension for a relaxation reset.

Respect Diversity and Avoid Pain

It's important to keep diversity in mind when teaching this technique. Any muscle groups where flexion causes pain or spasms should be avoided. Give children the option to pass on certain muscle groups and to focus on any options that feel comfortable for them. Flexing muscles with PMR is designed to add a moment of tension that gets released, but it shouldn't cause pain or distress.

Seek Support if You Need It

If self-regulation is difficult for your child, seek support from your child's pediatrician or a mental health professional like a child psychologist or psychiatrist.

Colleen A. Patterson, MA, is a psychologist who has worked with children, teens, and families in hospital and school settings. She is an advocate for the science of reading and mental health. Ms. Patterson lives near Toronto, Canada. Visit @PsychBooksforKids on X and Facebook.

Brenda S. Miles, PhD, is a clinical pediatric neuropsychologist who works with children, teens, and families. She blends brain science with creativity to build programs and resources that support learning and mental health. Dr. Miles lives near Toronto, Canada. Visit brendamiles.com and @Psych4Thought on Instagram.

John Joseph is the illustrator of multiple #1 *New York Times* bestselling books. When he is not illustrating books for children, John is teaching Visual Arts at a local elementary school. John lives in Colorado. Visit johnjosephillustration.com and @John_Joseph_Art on Instagram.

The American Psychological Association works to advance psychology as a science and profession, as a means to improve health and human welfare. APA publishes books for young readers under its imprint, Magination Press. It's the combined power of psychology and literature that makes navigating life's challenges a little easier. Visit maginationpress.org and @MaginationPress on Facebook, X, Instagram, and Pinterest.

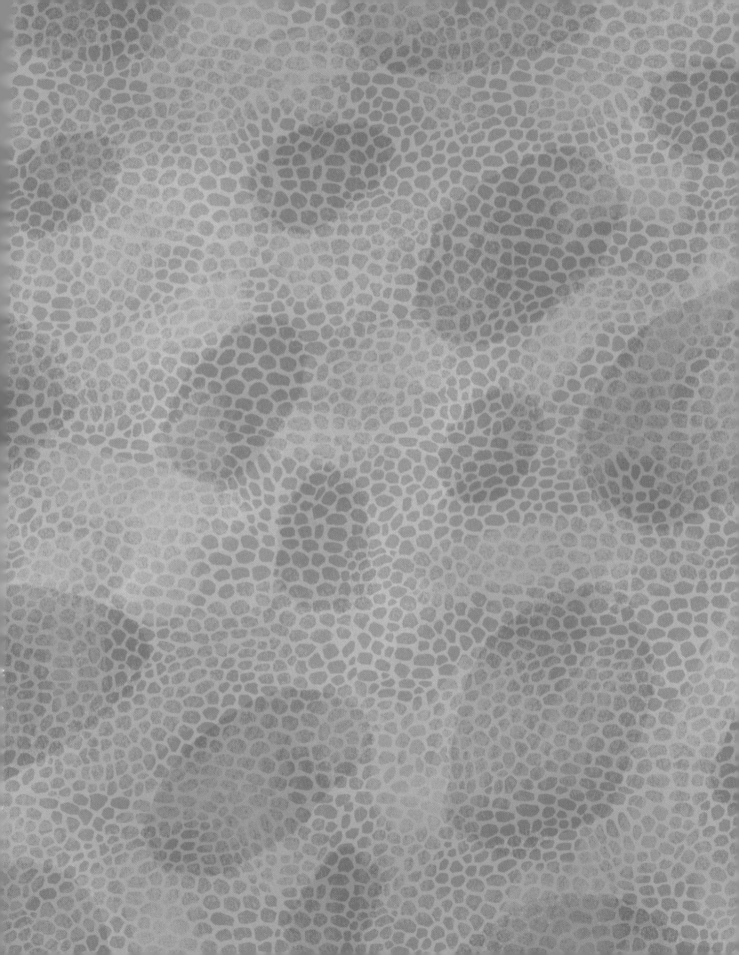

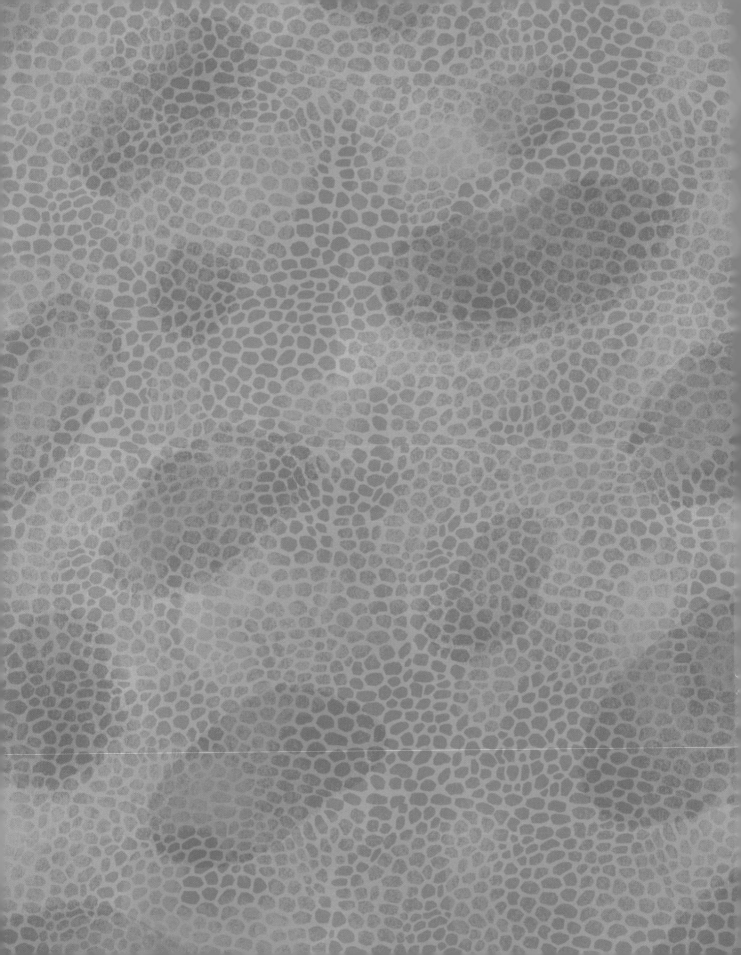